First published in Japan in 1981 by Child Honsha Co., Ltd. under the title *Nezumi no Densha*.
First published in the United States, Great Britain, Canada, Australia, and New Zealand in 2011
by North-South Books Inc., an imprint of NordSüd Verlag AG, CH-8005 Zürich, Switzerland.
Translated by Missy Debs and Masako Irie. Edited by Susan Pearson.
Distributed in the United States by North-South Books Inc., New York 10001.
Library of Congress Cataloging-in-Publication Data is available.
Printed in Germany by Grafisches Centrum Cuno GmbH & Co. KG, 39240 Calbe, November 2010.
ISBN: 978-0-7358-4012-6 (trade edition)
1 3 5 7 9 • 10 8 6 4 2

www.northsouth.com

FSC
Mixed Sources
Product group from well-managed
forests and other controlled sources

Cert no. SGS-COC-007065
www.fsc.org
©1996 Forest Stewardship Council

Seven Little Mice
Go to School

by Haruo Yamashita

illustrated by

Kazuo Iwamura

NorthSouth
New York / London

This is the story of seven little mice. They are septuplets, which is like twins only there are seven.

Tomorrrow the seven little mice will start school.

Mother has made them seven hats from bottle caps and seven book bags from cocoons and seven pairs of shoes from walnut shells. They looked very fine in their new outfits.

"Time for bed now," said Mother. "Tomorrow is a big day."

But the seven little mice didn't want to go to school. What a fuss they made.

"School is too far away!" "I'll be too sleepy to go to school!" "The wind will be so cold!" "We won't know anyone!" "There will be a bully!" "There will be a snake on the path!" "I don't want to go!"

Mother was worried. How was
she going to get her seven little
mice through the forest to school?
Then she had an idea.

That night she rolled two balls of blue yarn
through the forest, all the way to school.

"Put on your shoes and hats," said Mother
the next morning. "It's time for school!"
But the seven little mice paid no attention.

"All right," said Mother. "I will go alone."

Then she stood between the two lines of yarn and called out, "All aboard! The train for school is leaving now!"

"Wow! It's a train!" said the seven little mice, and they scurried to get ready for school. Then they lined up behind Mother, each one holding the tail of the mouse in front.

CHUG-CHUG-TOOT-TOOOOOOT.
The Mouse Train started through the forest.

Just as the Mouse Train was setting off, a wriggly snake came upon the yarn trail in the forest. "Hmmmm," said the snake. "Very interesting. I must see where this trail goes."

CHUG-CHUG-TOOT-TOOOOOOT.
The Mouse Train was moving fast, straight
into a dark tunnel.

And there was the wriggly snake!
"Oh, no!" said Mother, and she slammed
on the brakes. So did the seven little mice.

"Oh, no!" said the wriggly snake, and he
slammed on the brakes too. For what did he see?

Along the way, the Mouse Train had picked
up many more passengers, all on their way
to school. Now the train was ten times longer than the
wriggly snake.

"*Eeeeeeeek!*" cried the snake. "What a
loooooooooooong snake!"

And he turned around fast and slithered away.

Now the seven little mice happily go to
school every morning on the Mouse Train.
And who knows, maybe the train is chugging
along through the forest right now.